My "v" Sound Box®

Library of Congress Cataloging-in-Publication Data
Moncure, Jane Belk.
My "v" sound box / by Jane Belk Moncure; illustrated by Colin King.
p. cm.
Summary: A little girl fills her sound box with many words beginning with the letter "v."
ISBN 1-56766-788-0 (lib. reinforced : alk. paper)
[1. Alphabet.] I. King, Colin, ill. II. Title.
PZ7.M739 Myv   2000
[Fic]—dc21   99-056565

My "v" Sound Box®

Jane Belk Moncure

illustrated by Colin King

The Child's World®

Little  had a box.

"I will find things that begin
with my 'v' sound," she said.

"I will put them into my sound box."

Little found violets,

all kinds of very pretty violets.

She put some violets  into a vase.

Then she put the vase with
the violets

into her box.

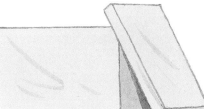

9

Next, Little  found

a piece of velvet,

very pretty velvet.

She made a velvet vest.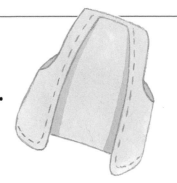

She put it on and pinned
a velvet bow on it.

She put velvet all around her box.
"What a very pretty box," she said.

Little  found a veil.

It was made of lace.

"Oh," she said.
"I can make something
with my violets and velvet

and lace veil."

Do you know what Little  made?

She made  valentines,

very nice   valentines.

Then she found a valentine verse.

Roses are red.
Violets are blue.
Sugar is sweet.
So are you!

She wrote the verse on her valentines.

Then she filled her box with valentines.
She pasted valentines all around
the box.

But some valentines fell out.

"What shall I do with all these valentines?" she said.

"I will send the valentines to my friends."

Then Little  had a very good idea.

She wrote another verse on each valentine:

Come to my party at one, for Valentine's Day fun.

She put the valentines into envelopes.
She put her friends' names and
addresses on the envelopes.
There were very many.

Little  got into her van
and drove to the mailbox.

When Little  got back home, she

got out the vacuum.

She used the vacuum to clean up the scraps of velvet and valentines.

On Valentine's Day,
her friends came
to her party.
Each one brought
valentines.

Little  and her friends made

valentine hats.

They put on their valentine hats
and played some games.

Then they opened the valentines.

valentine hats

velvet vest

vase of violets

valentine box

What fun they had at . . .

valentine hats

valentine placemat

velvet runner

valentine cake

the Valentine's Day party!

Can you read these words

with Little  ?

vegetables

volleyball

violin

vine

volcano

vitamins

vampire

vinegar

valley

ABOUT THE AUTHOR AND ILLUSTRATOR

Jane Belk Moncure began her writing career when she was in kindergarten. She has never stopped writing. Many of her children's stories and poems have been published, to the delight of young readers, including her son Jim, whose childhood experiences found their way into many of her books.

Mrs. Moncure's writing is based upon an active career in early childhood education. A recipient of an M.A. degree from Columbia University, Mrs. Moncure has taught and directed nursery, kindergarten, and primary grade programs in California, New York, Virginia, and North Carolina. As a former member of the faculties of Virginia Commonwealth University and the University of Richmond, she taught prospective teachers in early childhood education.

Mrs. Moncure has travelled extensively abroad, studying early childhood programs in the United Kingdom, The Netherlands, and Switzerland. She was the first president of the Virginia Association for Early Childhood Education and received its award for outstanding service to young children.

A resident of North Carolina, Mrs. Moncure is currently a full-time writer and educational consultant. She is married to Dr. James A. Moncure, former vice president of Elon College.

Colin King studied at the Royal College of Art, London. He started his freelance career as an illustrator, working for magazines and advertising agencies.

He began drawing pictures for children's books in 1976 and has illustrated over sixty titles to date.

Included in a wide variety of subjects are a best-selling children's encyclopedia and books about spies and detectives.

His books have been translated into several languages, including Japanese and Hebrew. He has four grown-up children and lives in Suffolk, England, with his wife, three dogs, and a cat.